THE SONG I'M IN

MAIJA BARNETT

An imprint of Enslow Publishing

WEST **44** BOOKS™

**Please visit our website, www.west44books.com.
For a free color catalog of all our high-quality books,
call toll free 1-800-398-2504.**

Cataloging-in-Publication Data

Names: Barnett, Maija.
Title: The song I'm in / Maija Barnett.
Description: New York : West 44, 2024. | Series: West 44
YA verse
Identifiers: ISBN 9781978596801 (pbk.) | ISBN
9781978596795 (library bound) | ISBN 9781978596818
(ebook)
Subjects: LCSH: American poetry--21st century. |
Poetry, Modern--21st century.| Poetry.
Classification: LCC PS584.B377 2024 |
DDC 811.008'09282--dc23

First Edition

Published in 2024 by
Enslow Publishing LLC
2544 Clinton Street
Buffalo, New York 14224

Editor: Caitie McAneney
Designer: Tanya Dellaccio Keeney

Photo Credits: Cover Sahara Frost/Shutterstock.com.

Printed in the United States of America

CPSIA compliance information: Batch #CS24W44: For further information contact
Enslow Publishing LLC at 1-800-398-2504.

*For Rob,
whose love and support made
this book possible.*

SKYLER, AGE 16

I am the girl
you cannot see.

The girl who hides
in her sister's
         shadow.

Face buried beneath a sheet
of hair.

I am the girl you
cannot hear.

The girl with the throat
of broken words.

Her voice is a bird's,
but she won't sing.

Instead she stares at the tops of her
ratty sneakers.

And tries to pretend
she isn't there.

DAD'S CALIFORNIA

That's where he is
with his
new life,
     new
          everything.

Golden foothills.
The pulsing beach.

We had the choice to
split—

I'd go with Dad.
Katy would stay
        with Mom.

But Katy said "No!"
and held my hand
till I thought it would
break.

We were 12
when it happened.

And we still looked
the same.

(Even Mom and Dad
got confused.)

But now I think
I should
        have gone.

If I had,
would I be a different
person?

DAD AND ME

It's not so much
the way
we look.

My hair and eyes are
just like
      Mom's.

It's how we think.
How we
      worry.

Before he left,
whenever I felt lost,

Dad was the one
who comforted me.

Mom always says,
"It's not so bad.
You just need to be
             positive."

She can't understand how
sometimes

when I open my eyes,
all I see is
      gray.

But when sadness eats me up
inside—

When fear and worry
make me freeze—

I don't need someone saying
I'm overreacting.

All I need is to talk
                    with Dad.

WHAT I HAVE

It's a strange word—
dermatillomania.
Der-muh-till-uh-MAY-nia.

Derma means skin.

Tillo means to pick.

And mania, well, that means
I can't stop.

It's not that I don't
want to.

It's just that something inside me
keeps saying
NO.

It all started when Dad
left.

I remember sitting in my room,
and finding a bump
on my chin.

It was just a pimple,
but it felt like
               more.

Then a calmness spread
through me.

I stopped thinking
about Dad.

When I looked up,
20 minutes had passed.

And the tips of my fingers
were coated
            in blood.

Jenna Hart.
Her name
still hurts.

Dad was the chef
at this Italian
                place.

And SHE
was the one
who handled
the wine.

Even though I see her
every summer,

I still don't think
she's okay.

Before he left,
Dad slept
on the couch.

Mom couldn't talk
without starting
to cry.

I would sit
on the swing
in our meadow.

Wildflowers scattered
through the grass
like stars.

I'd sing songs from the
radio.

14

Ones we'd learned
in school.

Katy sat beside me,
finding creatures
hidden in the clouds.

She told me my voice
took her somewhere—

a magical place
just for us.

Away from Mom's tears
and Dad's sad eyes.

Away from the moment Dad said
he was
            moving
                    away.

MOM'S BOYFRIEND, RAY . . .

is super nice.
Which makes him
hard to hate.

He builds websites.
And he's always calm and
very smart.

He ate at
Dad's Burlington restaurant
until he met Mom.

Then, even though it was
his favorite,
he wouldn't eat there
anymore.

I guess that's
devotion.

I guess that's
Ray.

Katy calls him our
Ray of sunshine.

Because he's always smiling
and making pancakes.

And saying he's glad we're in
his life.

TROY

Mom said Ray's wife
died of
cancer
when Troy was
              12.

Troy's 16 now—
just like Katy and me.

He's blond and thin and
rarely smiles.

He plays football and
is popular,

with clear blue eyes and
perfect skin.

Katy says she feels
bad for him.

It must have been hard
losing his mom
so young.

I feel bad, too.

But I wish he didn't
stare at my face all the time.

And I wish he and Katy
didn't always get along.

LATER

I'm propped on the
bathroom counter.

Trying to forget
what's to come.

I blink hard,
and then I see it.

My skin is scratched
                    raw.

Blood oozes from a sore
on my cheek.

And there's a gash
across my nose.

Oh god, I think.

How long have I been here?

*What have I
done?*

TORN

Ray and Troy
come over to pack up
more of our stuff.

Summer's ending.
And it feels like life is, too.

Katy's adapted.
I don't know how.

(I guess all her screaming
was just
for show.)

Last week she made varsity at
South Burlington High.

Mom and I watched
from the bleachers

as Katy stood guard at the
field hockey goal.

It hurt when I saw
Troy and his friends,

cheering her on
across the field.
When Mom asked why
I didn't join them,

I touched my face and
looked away.

How could I tell her
Katy *made* Troy
                invite me?

How could I admit
part of me wanted
                to go?

But another part,
the part that feared
                their glances,

kept me
next to Mom

and away
from the others.

MEDICATION: PROS AND CONS

One night, I go on Google
just to see
what could
        go wrong.

And, the truth is,
it's not
        great.

I've done this research before,
but I need
to check
before I make up
my mind.

I find the usual suspects:
stomachaches,
headaches,
extra sweating.

My chances of suicide
would go
way up.

And, to make things worse, I might
never sleep.

When I was younger,
I read that list and
         freaked.

But this time, I think:
this might stop my picking.

Then I close my eyes and
picture Katy.

I want my life to be like hers
again.

And with this medication,
maybe it could.

DRUGS

We're about to move out
when I tell Mom
I'll take
      the meds.

I can't do this.
Not anymore.
I need a fresh start
in my new town.

I stay in the car
while Mom gets
my prescription.

Fingers working
a hangnail
on my
      thumb.

It's a little thing,
but it keeps me
        calm.

When I check,
my nail is slick
with blood.

I hold my breath
and picture my sister.

I hope this will
be over
      soon.

JEALOUSY

Katy is
beautiful.

Her soft skin
glows
like 1,000 stars.

She looks like me
if I were someone else.

Someone who
didn't pick.

I don't want to be jealous,
but I can't
           stop.

She says my voice
makes me
special.

But I would trade it for the way
people smile
           at her.

MEDS

I hold the pill in
my hand
and wonder how something
so small
can make
a difference.

I down my first pill
the morning we move.

Trying not to think about
what could go
                           wrong.

Instead, I focus on
saying goodbye.

To our house.
To our field.
To our lonely swing.

To the silver birches that sway
in the wind.

My world is
changing,
but, for once, I have hope.

Even if it comes in the shape
of a pill.

SHARING A ROOM

We're at Ray's house,
sharing the guest room.

Ray was all smiles
when we moved in.

I like Ray's laugh.
The way he made his home
ours.

He put Mom's fern
in the kitchen window.

Stacked our plates
in the cabinet, too.

It's only Troy who's
stayed
silent.

His hard eyes
follow me
wherever I go.

I try to forget him,
as night creeps in,
and Katy's breath
fills the room.

This is the 10th time
I've laid here
sleepless.

(I guess some of those
side effects
were true.)

I stare out the window
at the lonely streetlight.

And count the hours
until
                    it's day.

CALLING WHITNEY
IN MY HEAD

It's another night and
I'm awake.

Whitney's voice
oozes
from my earbuds.

I imagine asking her
about
not sleeping.

Seeing how long she thinks
I should let it
                    go.

"Skyler," she'd coo,
her words velvet and honey.

"The only one who can decide that
 is you."

TALKING WITH MOM

There's a week left
of summer

when Mom
corners me.

We're alone
in the kitchen.

"Skyler," she says.
"I'm concerned."

I nod because
I understand.

The dark semicircles under my eyes
bloom like lilies.

Proof that sleep
rarely comes.

"My skin's better," I say,
which is true.

I haven't picked
in a week.

"But you're not sleeping," says Mom.
"And school's about to start.
How are you going to
                              cope?"

DR. MARTIN SAYS . . .

"Give it two more weeks.
If you still aren't sleeping,
we'll change things up."

Mom's there for the call,
and she agrees.

I stare at my tired face
on the screen,

relieved to see
the rawness gone.

FAMILY TIME?

Troy and Ray are in the den
watching football.

(Mom and Katy
aren't home.)

"Hi, Skyler," says Ray.
"Want to watch the game?'

I'm about to say yes,
even though I'm not
into sports.

(Ray's so nice,
I hate turning him
                down.)

Then I see Troy's eyes turn to
stone. He doesn't want me here.

"That's okay," I mumble,
and hurry upstairs.

I sit in my room
and think of
                home.

KATY'S PLAN

"You seem bummed," says Katy,
back from
practice.

She flops onto her bed
and stares
        at me.

"Is it the meds?" she asks.
"Or are you nervous
about starting
        school?"

"Both," I say.
"I've been thinking.
Maybe I should move in
with Dad?"

"Right," scoffs Katy.
"Like you'd do that.
Besides, do you really want Jenna
as your
fake mom?"

I force a fake laugh
because she's right.

I'd never leave my sister.

"Wait," says Katy.
"I have something
for you."

She pulls out
her phone.

"I made you a playlist," she says,
typing a few things,
sending me the list.
"Beyoncé and Whitney
and the rest.
Why don't you learn to sing the songs
like the original singers?
Maybe it will help."

I pick up my own phone with shaky
hands. Browse the list.

Then, without thinking,
I hug my sister.

She knows me
better than anyone.

STARTING SCHOOL

The first three weeks crawl by.

Whitney and Mariah's
"When You Believe"
is my anthem.

I hope their promise about miracles
is true.

My classes are fine.
I'm in middle-level everything.

The only one that's hard is
math.

At lunch, I sit at a table
with Katy and Troy.

It's all the sports kids,
and they laugh and joke.

I feel like a shadow,
watching the clock.

Waiting for time
                    to disappear.

SINGING HELPS

I have to hand it to Katy—
she was right.

Each afternoon, I listen to the
playlist.

I do it when Mom and Ray
are at work.

And Katy and Troy are still at
practice.

The house is an
empty stage

waiting to be filled
with music.

And the best part is
last night I slept!

FAMILY MEETING

It's Sunday night
when Mom
enters
our bedroom.

Dad's on
speakerphone.
So it's serious.

"Skyler," says Mom,
touching my arm.
"Katy has something
to say."

My stomach drops,
and I stare at
my sister,
who looks like she
wants to hide.

"I can't sit with you
at lunch," whispers Katy.

"What?" I ask.
Katy starts to cry.

"Skyler," says Dad.
"Listen to your sister.
You need to hear
how she feels."

"I love you," says Katy.
"But I need
space.

You act like you hate
the entire table.
Everyone's asking
what's wrong."

Mom says, "I already spoke
with the school.
Tomorrow you're eating
somewhere
        else."

"But I don't know anyone!"
My insides hurt.
Now everyone will think
I'm a freak—if they don't already.

"Sky?" says Dad.
"You'll be
        fine, honey."

His voice comes out
scratchy and
          small.
Like he doesn't believe it.

"Why? Am I too much of a loser
to sit with Katy?"
I say.
My words are
acid.
I'm terrified of what they're
making me do.

"No," says Dad.
"You just need to find
your people.

And guess what?
Now's your chance."

Not even Dad is on my side.
I leave the room,
and realize there's no safe place
or person
anymore.

MY PEOPLE

Ms. Figgs,
the school guidance counselor,
finds me before lunch.

She's short and plump
and looks 18.

"Skyler!" she squeaks.
Her smile
is warm.

"I've got some people
for you to meet."

I follow her down the
crowded hall.
This is so embarrassing.

She tells me
my hair
matches
one of her cats.

I try to laugh,
but panic is
shooting through me.

My hand skids nervously across
my chin.
Before I can even think about
picking,
Ms. Figgs turns and says,
"We're here!"

She leads me into a
tiny office.

It's windowless and packed with
books.

Two girls sit hunched over a table
playing UNO.

Oh no, I think,
itching to run.

FRIENDS?

Lisa James and Harmony Cook
couldn't be more different
if they tried.

Lisa is tall with long, black hair
tied in a
       ponytail.

She wears thick glasses.

She can also
really
       draw.

That first day in
Ms. Figgs's office,

she lets me flip though
her sketchbook.

I can't believe what's
             there.

The best is the picture of
Harmony.

Her wild hair has words
hidden inside.

Talkative, funny—
gets what she wants.
That's a true description.

Harmony never stops
                          talking.

(It's probably because
she has dreams.)

Harmony wants braces
to fix her
          buckteeth.

And a bigger apartment
for her mom.

This all tumbles out
the first day we meet.

(Harmony's a self-proclaimed
oversharer.)

But I think she's just honest
and brave.

The thing I like most about
these two,

is they don't say anything about
my skin.

They just smile
and let me sit at their table,

a fan of UNO cards
in my hand.

Ms. Figgs works silently
at her desk.

I'm sure she's listening,
but I don't care.

I've just found a life raft
in the ocean of
                high school.

Two fellow survivors
to help me through
                the year.

THAT DAY AFTER SCHOOL

Troy and Katy are in the kitchen
doing homework

when I come in
for a snack.

They're always together now
without me.

"Skyler?" says Katy.
"How'd it go today?"

Her eyes say,
Forgive me.

Troy's eyes say
something
           else.

TROY AND I

don't get along.

It's not that we fight
exactly.

It's more like we're
distant moons.

And Katy's our planet.

We orbit around her.
Painfully
        polite.

Except when I feel his eyes
on my broken skin.

Then anger
        sizzles
                inside me.

And I imagine how it'd feel
to punch him
in the
        face.

"You're lucky," says Lisa.
"Your mom's so cool."

"Yeah," I nod.
Because she is.

We hang at Harmony's
on the weekends
for three weeks
straight.

It's a tiny,
single-bedroom apartment.
(Harmony's mom sleeps on the
couch.)

But even though Lisa's place has a
hot tub,

and my house is big enough for
five—

it's Harmony's mom
who leaves money for pizza.

It's this place
where we feel at home together,
just having fun.

MATH WITH LISA

Lisa and I
have math together.

Geometry—
not my favorite
at all.

But Lisa draws
cartoons
on all her assignments.

And though she's quiet,
she makes me
                laugh.

Mr. Rumple, our teacher,
doesn't think we're
funny.

But Lisa made my
test scores shoot
way up.

Her silly drawings
help me remember.

And her friendship
makes me love
that class.

NOT PICKING

The meds are working,
but I think it's more
than that.

(I haven't picked in
several weeks.)

My voice is stronger,
though I still
sing
     alone.

When everyone is
gone.

But my heart
is glowing
with this new life
of mine.

My friends.
My school.
Finally fitting in.

The only hard parts
are missing Katy
and hiding my scars,

which are still here.

HAPPY

I'm home alone
singing along to
Katy's playlist.

Whitney and Dionne Warwick's
"That's What Friends Are For"
comes on.

My voice rises
with theirs.

And so does
         my heart.

I think of Harmony and Lisa,
and decide to tell them.

They've never said anything
about my skin,
but I'm ready
for them
     to know.

"They'll understand," croons Whitney
inside my head.

I smile because
I think so, too.

GROUP CHAT

Harmony texts
during math.

Meet at lunch.
I've got a plan!

Hallway B.
Beneath the stairs.

BE THERE.
You two are gonna
LOVE this!!!

BENEATH THE STAIRS
IN HALLWAY B, PART 1

Harmony smiles.
"Lisa?
 Skyler?"

Her bunny teeth
and her honest excitement
make me like her
              even more.

"I know what we have to do."

"What?"
Lisa sounds uncertain.

I lean against
the floor-length window.

Warm and bright beneath the
stairs.

Harmony says,
"Let's all try out for the
school musical!"

Lisa gasps, and I freeze.

"Come on," pleads Harmony.
"It'll be fun! And we have to do it together.
Then we'd have built-in friends
in the cast."

PROBLEMS

I stare out the window
on the bus ride home.

Watching the world
blur by.

Colorful leaves litter
the roadside.

The trees have become
something new.

I used to watch the seasons change
in wonder.

But now my mind is
somewhere else.

How can I help Lisa
and not hurt Harmony?

And how do I get out of
auditioning?

Because the one thing I know
is that I don't need people

watching me.

Wondering what's wrong with
my skin.

And I still haven't told my friends
about my
       dermatillomania.

I close my eyes and try to
decide
       what to do.

BENEATH THE STAIRS IN HALLWAY B, PART 2

I'm dreading lunch
and only Katy
knows why.

Yesterday, after
we made up,
she told me
what to
        do.

"Just tell them everything," said Katy.
"You said you were planning to
anyway."

I shuffle down the
busy hallway.

The October sun
turns the walls
                gold.

My friends are waiting
under the staircase.

I'd texted them I had
something to say.

"Hi." My voice cracks
when I greet them.

I look out the window
at the
falling leaves.

72

Then it all comes
rushing out.

"Harmony,
I'll go to the audition,
but I'm not going
on stage.
It's just . . .
You two never said
anything,
but I have a skin-picking
disorder.
I'm not ready to be
in front of people
like that."

They're both quiet, and then—

"Okay," says Harmony, with a shrug.
"Lisa said she's
gonna do it.
You can just be
moral support."

"You're auditioning?"
I turn to Lisa,
surprised.

She nods, and shoots me
a brave smile.

"Thanks for telling us
about your skin," says Lisa.

Then both of my friends
give me a
             hug.

TALKING WITH LISA

"Why did you change your mind?"
I ask Lisa
while we're walking
to math.

"Why did you tell us
about your skin?" she says.

"Because you're my friends,"
I answer.
"And I need you to
be there
       for me."

"That's the same reason," says Lisa,
"that I agreed to
try out with Harmony."

TRYOUTS

The velvet curtains
shiver on the stage.

Ms. Lawrence,
the chorus teacher,

barks directions
from the piano.

"Next!" she calls,
her voice an operatic
                soprano.

Brown hair twisted in a
messy French braid.

Lisa sings . . .
I think.

Her voice is a
whisper.

And I can tell she
wants to
        hide.

Harmony is loud
and way off-key.

But you can't beat her
                enthusiasm!
I tap my feet to the songs
but lock my voice
inside.

Wishing I were brave enough to
take the stage.

I know I sing better than anyone
here.

Why am I so afraid to
get up there?

KATY

Even though Katy and I
made up,

she still spends
most of her time
with Troy.

Every weekend,
there are parties.

And at lunch,
she and Troy still
sit with the jocks.

They're a bunch of loud boys in
baseball hats.

And girls in team sweatshirts,
with mostly blond hair.

I keep telling myself
Katy's not
        like them.

She's just trying
to be
     cool.

NOT A
SECRET ANYMORE

"You told Ms. Lawrence
about my singing?"
I hiss
after hearing the news.

"I had to," says Harmony.
"You're just so good!
I couldn't keep that
to myself."

"You should have asked," I say.
"It wasn't your secret
to tell."

"I'm sorry!"
Harmony looks like she's
about to cry.
"But you sounded just like
the people on Broadway.
Why would you keep that
to yourself?"

AN OFFER

Ms. Figgs finds me
during
      lunch.

"Skyler," she says,
pulling me
from
my friends.

Harmony's mouth
makes a silent
Oh.

"Mind if we
have a
chat?"

Ms. Figgs leads me
into her
messy office.

I take the chair
across from
        her.

"I've spoken with
Ms. Lawrence," she says,
tucking some hair
behind her ear.
"She heard
you can
      sing."

ALMOST LIKE WHITNEY

I use GarageBand
to record myself.

And do "I Will Always Love You,"
almost like Whitney
but with my own flair.

I close my eyes when I sing
and think of Dad.

When I told him
about this,

he said he was
proud.

And you know what?
I'm proud, too.

WOW!

I got in!
I can't believe it.

Ms. Lawrence says
I have a future in vocal performance.

When I hear that,
I forget my skin.

For the first time,
I feel so happy
to be
        me!

STRENGTH

I'm safe beneath
a layer of
makeup

when I walk through
the chorus room doors.

Ms. Lawrence points me to
the mezzo-sopranos.
Even though I have a
wide range.

The other kids stare.
Then the piano
                    starts.

I open my heart and
let the song
                in.

I don't sing the solo.
But I know
            I could.

Right now,
with this melody
rising inside me,

I feel like I'm finally
part of something.

ANOTHER ANNOUNCEMENT

Mom and Ray
sit us down.

They say it's important,
which makes me
scared.

Mom's eyes
glow
like a cat's.

She smiles at Ray
and grabs
his hand.

Sunshine Ray gleams
like the
            moon.

Then says in a voice
full of
            joy:

"Katy, Skyler, my dearest
                        Troy.

June and I have something to
say."

"We're getting MARRIED!"
shouts Mom.

Her voice goes
high.

"Wow!" says Katy,
breaking into a
                grin.

"That's great!" says Troy.
He gives Ray a
                hug.

Though, for a second,
his eyes look
sad.

I sit
in total silence.

My insides
turn
to ice.

OVER

Tonight I stand at the
bathroom mirror

and try not to think about
Mom and Ray.

My fingers
slip
across my face

as I wait for the
numbness
to come.

"Stop it!" I hiss,
shoving my fists
into my pockets.

Why can't I just
be happy,
like Katy?

I like my life
and my friends.
My new place
in Bella Voce.

My picking is
under
          control.

NEW PLAN

Today I meet with
Dr. Martin,

and I tell her the truth—
I'm worried
about
picking again.

"What's changed?" she asks.

I explain about the
wedding.
How I'm not ready
for another huge
change.

"Skyler," says Dr. Martin,
when I'm finished,
"think of everything
you've accomplished
                    so far."

We talk about
friends,
how I love
Bella Voce.

How I use music
to escape.

When we're done,
Dr. Martin gives me
an assignment.

She asks me
to write
a song.

"Music," she says,
"is how you connect
with your feelings.
Writing could help you
find acceptance."

The moment she says it,
a warmth rushes
through me.

In my heart,
a flower
          blooms.

MY SONG – A CAPPELLA (JUST VOICE)

No one sees me,
yet I'm still here.

When I feel their stares,
I won't disappear.

My heart turns cold,
and I want to cry.

But I'll fight to love.
I'll work to fly.

Because I'm not empty.
I'm not lost.

Though the path I'm hunting for
is covered in moss.

My friends are my beacon.
I'll fight for their light.

I hold warmth in my heart—
I'm not scared of the night.

THOUGHTS

I wrote that in
one
sitting
in a new notebook.

And I'm
            proud.

Except for the
moss part.

(I'm not sure about
that.)

But writing kept my
hands
busy.

My brain
working.

My heart
hot
in my chest.

It saved me from
getting lost
in the bathroom mirror.

From a face that's bleeding
and full of
            sores.

I want to sing it
for Katy,
but she's with Troy.

So I call Dad
                instead.

WAIT FOR IT . . .

Dad loved it!
He cried when I was done.

He even liked the moss part.
Who knew?

SHARING

It's Monday morning,
and I bring my song
to school.

I recorded it on
GarageBand
and put it on
my phone.

At lunch, I'll play it
for
Lisa and Harm.

I can't believe how excited I am
to show them this huge
piece of me.

BETRAYED

I'm in a bathroom stall
before lunch
when I hear them—

Emily and Julie
from Bella Voce.

(They're popular girls
who do sports AND sing.)

I recognize Emily's
soprano.

And Julie's deeper
tones.

"I don't even get why she's in,"
complains Emily.
"It's not like she auditioned
like the rest
                    of us."

"And what's up with her face?"
Julie says.

My stomach sinks.
They're talking about
                    me.

"I know!" scoffs Emily.
"Who wears makeup
like that?
It's not like it's hiding
anything."

Their voices are
poisonous vines

crawling across
the floor.

I hold my breath
and hope no one
hears me,

awaiting my chance
to escape.

Then the door
bangs,
and two more girls
enter.

"Hi, Harmony," says Emily.

God, I hate Emily's voice.
So sweet and strong
during chorus.
Now it's something
                else.

I peek under the
bathroom stall.

There's Harmony's blood-red
Converse.

And Lisa's in her
                yellow Crocs.

My heart leaps.

My friends are here!

"Aren't you two friends with
Skyler Reeds?"
Julie asks, sweetly.

Her tone
makes me
want to
        scream.

"Maybe," says Harmony,
nervously.

(Even though she's fearless
with me and Lisa,
the popular kids
make her
        sweat.)

"Well, we were just wondering,"
Emily jumps in.

There's a crack
above the hinge
of the stall's door.

I press my eye to it,
and see the back of Julie's head.
Neat brown hair—
a perfect braid.

"We don't get her,"
says Emily.

I spot her glossy
curls.

(Her face is hidden
from view.)

"It's just gross that she wears
so much makeup," adds Julie.
"It's not like we can't tell
what's underneath."

"What do you mean?"
asks Harmony.

Lisa stays silent.

"Her scars," Emily giggles,
her voice
a knife.
"I mean, who is she kidding,
anyway?"

"Right," says Harmony,
and then she
                        laughs.

Hot tears
flood my cheeks
in shame.

ALONE AGAIN

Harmony keeps texting about meeting
for lunch.

And when Lisa tried joking
during math,
I pretended she wasn't there.

I'm not speaking to them.
And I'm not going to chorus.

Even though Ms. Lawrence
has emailed me twice.

Yesterday, Ms. Figgs pulled me
from English and asked
what was wrong.

But I don't care.
Not anymore.

All I want, is to

d
i
s
a
p
p
e
a
r.

DROWNING

I'm sitting alone
in my bedroom.

Trying to decide
what to do.

My stomach hurts,
and my mind feels buzzy.

Full of everything
I've lost.

I haven't spoken to my friends
in over a week.

I've avoided our
hangouts.

Ignored them in the
halls.

I know they're wondering
what happened,

but it hurts too much
to say.

Each day feels like I'm
inhaling water.

And no matter how hard
I try,

I *never*
get enough
air.

LYING

One night, Katy asks
what's
      wrong.

We're lying in bed
on either side of the room.

The darkness between us,
impossible to cross.

I want to tell her,
but nothing
  comes out.

Instead, I stare out the window
at the lonely streetlight.

And pretend I'm
             fine.

LOST

I start picking
again.

(I don't mean to.)

But it's the only way
I can *not*
        feel.

My face is blotchy
and raw.

But my heart is worse.

And so is
        my pride.

Why did things have to
get so good,

if I was going to lose everything
in the
        end?

WANTING WHAT'S FAKE

Home is where
people plan weddings.
And ask why I'm
picking my skin.

Mom thinks that we should
up my medication dose.

That I should tell Dr. Martin
how I feel.

But all I do is
block my friends' numbers.
And hide from Troy's
watchful glare.

I wish I could return to
when I was almost
                    happy.

Even if it was probably
completely
            fake.

TROY WHEN NO ONE'S LOOKING

It's midnight, and
I can't sleep.

So I slip into the kitchen
for a snack.

I'm about to open the fridge
when I see him.

Troy— alone
in his ratty pajamas.

Sobbing into a glass
of milk.

I know why he's here.

Today was his mother's
birthday.

Ray didn't make a big deal.
No one did.

But maybe burying this day
deep inside

wasn't the best thing
for Troy.

He looks up
when he sees me.

I'VE MADE
A DECISION

I'm standing at the
bathroom mirror—

not picking my face.
Though my cuticles are
                    raw.

When I met with Dr. Martin today,
I kept my thoughts
                    to myself.

I don't want anyone to guess
what I'm about to do.

What I have to do.

AFTER SCHOOL
THE NEXT DAY

I try calling Dad.

His cell rings and rings.
Then goes to
                    voicemail.

Once that happens,
I just hang up.

Then I stare at my reflection
in my darkened phone.

Hoping I'm making
the right
            choice.

SNEAKY LIAR

When you've practiced
for years
being quiet and invisible,
it's not so tricky
to be a thief.

All you have to do is
lie
and
sneak.

No one would imagine
you would sneak into your
soon-to-be stepbrother's
bedroom.

Not to borrow his calculator,
but because you want
the bank card

buried in his wallet.

He's at football practice,
but his wallet isn't.

You know this because
you overheard him talking
with his dad.

About how all his friends
know
his locker combination.
So maybe the bank card
would be safer
at home.

And of course Sunshine Ray agreed.
So it's here.

Ready to be plucked,
like a ripe piece of
fruit.

And that's exactly
what
        I do.

THE PURCHASE

I made the purchase for
tonight.

Got my tickets.
Stuffed in my bag.

It's a colorless
Saturday evening.

Rain splatters the November
grass.

Troy and Katy are at a
game.

Mom and Ray went to dinner
and a movie.

Mom gave me a hug
before she left.

Asked if I wanted to tag
along.

I fake yawned and
shook my head.

A wave of red hair slicing across
my eyes.

LEAVING

My skin is a mess.
But the night doesn't care.

It hides me better than
foundation.

I slip on my raincoat.

Pick my backpack
up.

Leave my lyrics notebook behind.

Now, I'm ready to
go.

It's an hour's walk to
Burlington International.

My connecting flight to New York
leaves at midnight,
and it's 9:00 PM.

After I get there,
I'll have two hours to
check in.

I take a deep breath
and don't look back.

ALMOST

I'm on Kennedy Drive
when lights
blind me.

The car swerves so close
I freeze.

Or my mind does.

But my body knows
what to do.

I dive to the right,
into a
         ditch.

My pulse throbs.
I'm covered in mud.

But the car
races on.

The driver doesn't even know
what they've almost
                        done.

DOUBT

I can't help but wonder
if the car
was a sign.

Maybe this isn't the right move
after all?

I stand on the side of the
empty road
            and call Dad again.

But, of course,
he doesn't pick up.
Maybe he doesn't love me
anymore either.

"Dad?" I whisper
to the sheets of
rain.

To the limp grass.

To the darkness around
me.

"Dad— I need you.
Help me, please!"

My body is covered in
scratches and bruises.

But it's really my heart
that hurts the most.

I HATE FLUORESCENTS

I hate them because
they show

EVERYTHING.

They're a terrible eye
that nothing can hide
                    from.

When I walk into the airport,
I find a bathroom
fast.

Then I grab paper towels.

Soak them
in water.

Wipe off the mess
as best I can.

An old lady walks in,
but I ignore her.

Though I can feel her
staring
at my skin.

I know what she sees:
I'm raw
       and bloody.

We both know
something's
                wrong.

But I focus on
pulling out
my potions.

And dabbing them
everywhere.

It takes a while.
But I need this
protection.

Like a charm in a
fairy tale.

The kind with
dragons and princesses,

where everything
works out
in the end.

Yes, it's happily ever after
that I'm
                after.

I think of Whitney,
with her magical voice.

And hope I can make
everything
        right.

MY HEART STOPS
WHEN I SEE THEM

I step out of the
restroom and there they are.

Waiting,
like they knew where I was
all along.

Katy and Troy.

I'm a deer that's caught
in headlights,
and I don't know
where to go.

Then Katy
runs
toward me.

Eyes red
from tears.

"Skyler!" she screams.

I ache for her
                    hug.

But instead
I step back.

Pull away from
my sister.

My twin.
My other half.

I'm leaving this time.

Going where I belong.

And she can't
stop me.

KATY LOOKS HURT

"What?"
I ask, my voice sharp.
"Why are you even here?"

The fluorescents
burn my face.

I know they're showing
every spot.

Every pore.

Every layer of
foundation.

Thick and painted and
oh-so fake.

"Skyler?" says Katy, her voice breaking.

Her voice breaks something
inside me, too. I ask,

"How did you know
where to find me?"

TROY STANDS
BESIDE HER

He takes a step closer
and holds out
                his phone.

"What?" I snap.

But I
    see it.

Bright and white—
the digital receipt.

All $525 dollars of it.

My one-way ticket to
                San Francisco.

"You're leaving," says Katy.
"You're running away."

My voice catches
when I speak.

"Yes," I whisper.
"Yes, I am."

"Does Dad know?" asks Katy.

"Does it matter?" I ask.
My green eyes
catch hers.

And that's when I see
she's about to
                    cry.

"Skyler," says Troy.

*Why does he have to
be here?*

"Can we have
a minute?"

"I can't," I say.
"I have to check in."

I point to the empty
metal detector.

The conveyor belt that the luggage
goes through.

The bored security guards.

"It won't take long,"
says Troy.
"Then neither of us
will stop you.
If you still want to
go."

Katy shoots him a look,
eyebrows raised.
Then she nods
and sighs.

ANGER THROBS IN ME

I clench my
jaw.

"Please," says Troy,
begging now.
"Come on, Skyler, give me
one chance."

The airport's practically empty.

Even the old woman
from the restroom
is nowhere
    to be found.

It's 10:00 PM, and I'm taking the
red-eye to New York.
Then catching the first morning flight
to San Francisco.

I know I have time,
but I don't want
            to talk.

"For me?" asks Katy.

I glare at my sister—
a happier, healthier version
of me.

"Fine," I whisper.

TIME FOR BATTLE?

We're sitting on the benches
by the tall glass doors of the airport.

I'm on one bench.
Katy and Troy
are on another.

It feels like I'm heading
into battle.

Troy's face is set,
but his eyes are
                    sad.

Katy sits quietly
beside him.

Then nudges him with
her toe.

"Skyler," says Troy,
peering at me.

He takes a deep breath,
and starts to
                    talk.

TROY'S APOLOGY

"Skyler, I'm sorry about
what I said.
That thing about
your face.
I didn't mean it.
I was just so
embarrassed and angry
about you catching me crying
like that.
It's just that . . ."

Troy looks away,
his eyes
filling with
tears.

". . . sometimes it feels like
we're erasing *my*
                    mother.

Once you two moved in,
she really felt . . .
gone."

Troy runs a hand
through his
hair.

Takes a deep breath
and continues on.

"You know," says Troy,
glancing away,

"I haven't seen my dad this happy
in a long time.

I just don't want him
to forget
our other life.
The one with just
my mom and me."

Silence.

Troy stares
at me.

"Anyway, Skyler . . ."

His voice is soft.

"I'm sorry.
I really am."

HOW I FEEL

I feel sorry for Troy.
I do.

But I hate the way
he watches
          me.

How he never
lets me in.

Not the way he does
with Katy.

"That's not it," I say.

And I look him in the
eyes.

Daring him to see
my imperfections.

Daring him to accept
that part
       of me.

MY TURN

"Skyler!" warns Katy.

"No," I say.
"It's my turn to speak."

It's time for me
to use my voice.

I glare at Troy.
He's gnawing his bottom lip.
But I don't care if he's
nervous.
I need him
to know.

"Ever since we met," I say,
"you've left me out.
You are always
such a
                    jerk."

Tears come.
But I blink them
                    away.

This is my chance to say how I feel.

"You only like Katy,
because she looks *right*
to you. She's popular.
You never
even bothered
to get to know
                    me."

136

Troy holds up his hands.

I see a flash
of sadness.

Mixed with a flash
of remorse.

"I know what I did,"
he whispers.
"And I know
I was wrong.
But I'd never met anyone
like you before.
And when kids at school
asked,
I didn't know
what to say."

"Because of my skin?"
I ask.
"A lot of kids have
skin problems
in high school."

Troy swallows.
"It was more than that.
You're so shy. Sensitive.
You don't act like
anyone I know."

"You mean I don't drink and
do sports?"

Troy blushes.

"Well," he says,
rubbing his hands together.
As if, suddenly,
he's feeling
        cold.

"I figured I could be friends
with Katy," he says.
"My dad would
like that.
But I couldn't find a way
to connect
        to you."

DO OVER

Troy hunches forward
and holds out his hand.

I know what he wants
me
to do.

"You're going to be
my sister,"
he says.
"Is there any way we can
start over?
Could you forgive
what I've done?"

The fluorescents are
beating down
              on him, too.

Highlighting the circles
beneath
       his eyes.

The sadness
on his face.

I see a boy
who misses
his mother.

Who knows
he's losing
something, too.

WHY I TAKE TROY'S HAND

I take it because
I forgive him.

And I want things to be
okay.

I see Katy's hopeful eyes,
and I'm finally ready to go home.

All of us.

Together.

GOING HOME

We walk out of the airport,
completely silent.

But it's a good silence,
at least for now.

Katy holds my hand,
while I hold
      my breath.

And hope that what Troy said was
true.

That he and I can
really
forget our past.

And start over
with something
new.

MOM FINDS OUT

"Promise me,"
says Mom,
"you'll never do that again."

I close my eyes and
make myself promise.

FRESH START

I'm back at school.
It's late November.

The world's a slab of
gray on gray.

Ray got the money back
from my ticket.

Well, sort of
got it back.

Now Troy has a bunch of
miles.

I wonder where he'll decide
to go.

At school, I don't hang with
Katy and Troy.

They told me
I could.

Katy said
she wanted me to.

"But don't you need
your space?" I asked.
She made a face.
(Which I guess
was her answer.)

Though, deep down, I wonder
if she's telling
the truth.

But Troy was right.
I don't fit in with their group.

And maybe I don't want to.

MY SKIN
IS IMPROVING

I'm not sure why.

Maybe it's because
things are better
                  at home?

The three of us
study together now.

Troy, Katy, and me,
in the kitchen.

And Troy's stopped staring,
which is nice.

NOW IT'S
JUST SCHOOL

where I feel
          alone.

I'm still avoiding Ms. Figgs
and my old friends.

They've taken the hint and are
staying away.

Which hurts because
I want to make up.

I'm just not sure
I can.

TELLING DAD

I finally tell Dad
what I tried to do.

(Mom said
it should come
from me.)

But I'm hurt that he
ignored my call
that day
when I needed him.

He sighs,
then explains
why I couldn't
reach him.

"I dropped my phone
in the bathtub,"
he says.
"You should have given
Jenna
a call."

"Oh," I say.

Because I realize I've done
what I always do.

Every time someone does something
that hurts me,
I take it personally.

Even when their reason
isn't about me
at all.

Dr. Martin says I need to
change how I see things.
I guess it's time
to listen
to her advice.

DAD BREAKS OUR SILENCE

"You know, you're always
welcome here," Dad says.
"Just next time,
try not to steal."

"Okay," I say.
Then we laugh.

And I think of how
I love my dad.

And I think of how
I miss my dad.

How many of my issues
started when he left.

But it might be time
to accept where I am now.

Who I am now.

THE PLAN

Ms. Lawrence and Ms. Figgs
catch me
during lunch.

I'm sitting alone,
near a window.

Pretending I don't
care.

Ms. Figgs bounces over.

Her pink lipstick
makes her seem
younger
than usual.

Ms. Lawrence is wearing
her trademark
                    braid.

"Skyler,"
sings Ms. Lawrence.
"I have an
idea.
How would you like a solo
in the winter
       concert?

Ms. Figgs and I think it would
do you
　　　　good.

Plus, you know,
your voice is *really*
　　　　good.

It's time for people
to hear it."

THE SONG

For a moment
I sit there,
unsure
what to say.

The world
swirls past,
but I don't
see it.

Instead, my skin
prickles
with excitement.

My heart beats like a
captured bird's.

"What song?"
I ask.

"True Colors,'"
says Ms. Lawrence.

Her eyes sparkle,
and she smiles
              wide.

"It's a great song," says Ms. Figgs,
in her counselor voice.
"I think it's the perfect
one
    for you."

AT HOME
AND THINKING

I'm alone in the bathroom,
aching to pick.

I know why
I want to.

I know what's
bothering me.

Dr. Martin and I have been working on
replacement
behaviors.

We've tried this before,
but I never
        committed.

I was always
too upset.

But this time,
I keep my hands down
and start
        singing.

Since no one's home,
I let my voice
pour
through the bathroom.

Let it seep into
the tiled
          walls.

Slide up
the faucet.

Disappear down
                the drain.

I know why
I'm anxious.

It's the solo
thing.

Part of me
wants
to do it.

To show everyone
who I am.

But another part is
terrified.

I'll be under the lights
for everyone
              to see.
My scars will be there.
And my sores will,
                    too.

Then Whitney's voice
is in my mind—

giving me the advice
I need.

"This is your chance," she says,
to the red-haired girl
in the mirror.

Who tries to be invisible
whenever she can.

While always aching
to be seen.

WHAT I'D LIKE TO DO

I'd like to find
Lisa and Harmony

and tell them
how I
        feel.

But the thought of it
makes my
insides
        burn.

My palms go
sticky-slick.

They've stopped
talking to me.

They've given
                up.

And the friendship we had
has faded
        away.

I can feel
its ghost
when I trudge down
the halls.

An emptiness
I can't
        fill.

WHERE I SIT
AT LUNCH

Basically, I sit
               alone.

Filling my notebook
with song lyrics
I might not show anyone
ever.

Katy and Troy still invite me
to their table.

But I don't
want to go.

I'm not like them.
I need my own people.

I just wish there was a way
to get them
               back.

I just wish there was an easy way
to open up
               again.

DINNER

Mom and Ray went out
tonight.

So it's just
Katy, Troy, and me.

We make boxed
mac and cheese

and joke while we
cook it.

It feels good to be
part of the group.

"Here," says Troy,
passing me three
bowls.

I set them on the
kitchen table
and notice the way
he's looking at me.

Not like before.

Like I was some sort of
creature.

Instead, this time he just
sees me
for me.

DR. MARTIN'S ADVICE

Dr. Martin thinks I should talk
to my
          friends.

Find a way to make things
right.

She says we should try this
before upping my medication.

But the anger's still there,
hiding inside me.

And I don't know how to
let it
          go.

PRACTICING

Today I practice
my solo
for Troy and Ray.

It's my first time
singing
when they're home.

I close
my eyes

and let the music
glide through me.

The air around me
feels
       alive.

Ray cries
when I finish.

Troy says,
"Wow!
That was
       great!"

And I really think
he means it.

REHEARSAL

My palms sweat
when I enter the chorus room.

The risers are there—
empty and waiting.

The piano glares,
its mouth
full of
            teeth.

Then, Ms. Lawrence
walks in.

She grins
when she sees me.

"Are you ready?"
she asks.

I swallow hard
because here
they come.

Julie and Emily—
the bathroom
                mean girls.

They don't think I
deserve
to be here.

But this time—
I know
        I do.

SINGING

The piano starts
and I find
      myself.

Music rushes through me
like a
      wave.

I forget
who I am.

Forget what I've
gone through.

All I want to do
is sing.

AFTERWARD

Afterward,
even Emily and Julie
clap.

Their mouths are open.
Eyes wide.

I hear Julie whisper,
"I didn't know she sounded
like *that*."

BENEATH THE STAIRS IN HALLWAY B, PART 3

I stand by the picture window
and stare at the bright
December snow.

I hope that Harmony and Lisa
show.

They don't know I'm here.

But I don't care.

Katy and Troy convinced me
to do this.

They said I should
take a
            chance.

It won't be easy.
But it might be worth it.

FORGIVENESS

Harmony cries
when she sees me.

And Lisa does,
too.

"Skyler!" says Harm,
grabbing my hand.
"You're here!"

She squeezes
until
it hurts.

"It took us a while,
but we know why you're angry,"
says Harmony.

Lisa stares at her
shoes.

Then she glances up,
looks right at me.

"We should have
stood up for you
in the bathroom," Lisa says.
"We just got
scared."

"Of what?" I ask.

166

My eyes are starting
to tingle,
but I blink back
the tears.

"Julia and Emily are so popular,"
Harmony chimes in.
"Lisa's right.
We didn't know
                    what to
                              do."

My stomach knots.
I nod . . .
because I understand.

LISA SAYS

"By the way,
you missed the musical."

I nod.
I regret not being there
for my friends.

"It was REALLY bad,"
says Lisa.

Then we all laugh
together.

MY SKIN

I want to pick my skin.

I keep trying replacement behaviors—
singing,
writing songs.

But it's still so hard.
And I know why.

It's because of
the winter
            concert.

I know my part.
And the chorus does, too.

Their voices wrap around
mine.

Building something beautiful.
Something new.

After all these years of
hiding in the background,

I'm out front.

Am I ready?

ZOOM

"Hi Skyler,"
says Dr. Martin.

I try to smile.
Then I click off my filter
and wait to hear
what she'll say.

I'm not wearing any
makeup.

I want her
to see.

"Things were going better,"
I whisper.
"But now the concert is
coming up.
And I need help."

Dr. Martin nods,
and mentions upping
my medication.

I close my eyes.

I think about it.

Then I nod,
and say,
"Let's try."

170

TALKING

It's night
and we're lying
in our room.

The blue-black darkness
like a bruise.

"Skyler," says Katy,
her voice thin.

Like it's echoing from
far away.

"I'm proud of what you're doing,"
she says.

"What?" I say.
"Upping my meds?"

"Yeah, I guess," says my sister.
"You're brave to try.
But that's not why
I'm proud.
You quit hiding yourself
from everyone.
When you get on that stage
at the holiday concert,
you'll finally show everyone
who you are."

"I'm still wearing makeup,"
I say.

I run my hands over my
skin.

The bumps and scars
make me sad.

"Who cares?" says Katy.
"We all cover something.
But you don't have to
cover *everything*.
At least now
you're gonna
                sing."

SOON

It's late December.

Dad's tickets
are booked.

He says he and Jenna
can't wait to visit.

Can't wait to come to my concert.

Jenna, I think.

But I lock the thought
away.

Katy says we need to
accept her.

But Katy's good
at change.

And I'm
            not.

Though I suppose, this time,
I could give it a
                    try.

SURPRISE

The day before the concert,
I'm under Stairway B.

Just like old times
except
not quite.

Harmony's quiet,
which is strange.

I wonder what's
going on?

Then she nods and Lisa
pulls something
from her bag.

"We got these for you,"
Lisa says.

She hands me a package.

"Open it!" squeals Harm,
smiling her
bunny grin.

"Okay," I say.
And I rip at the paper,

dropping sheets of newsprint
on the floor.
When I see what it is,
I gasp.

174

"Whitney socks!" screams Harmony
before I can say anything.

On each side of the pair of
knee socks,

Whitney Houston's face stares up
at me.

"We know you like her," says Lisa,
grinning now.

"And we thought these might
bring you
            luck."

My love for my friends
swells
inside me.

I think they are
my sisters,
too.

BEFORE
THE CONCERT

"Be brave," Ms. Figgs squeaks,
still sounding
        too young.

I pull up my Whitney socks
and close my eyes.

Then I touch my face
and know
       I can do this.

TAKING THE STAGE

The stage lights
glow
bright and hot.

I spot
Dad and Jenna.

And
Mom and Ray.

Katy and Troy.

Harmony and Lisa.

I check my
Whitney socks.

Then I close my eyes
and prepare
to sing.

THE SONG I'M IN

The music rises—

gliding
       through
             me.

Flowing through
every bit
of air.

The stage lights
glow
like an ancient
sun.

And I can't
hide.

Not
anymore.

But I'm not sure
I even want to.

Because it doesn't matter
if my skin is
          raw.

Or that sometimes
I'm so lost,
I hide behind
my
   hair.

All that matters
is the sound
of my
        voice.

And the voices
behind me,

bleeding
into
    one.

I forget
what I look like.

Forget
who I am.

And then find
myself
        all over
                again.

MY BEAUTY

is
there,
inside
the music.

My breath
is the path
that guides me
       home.

FINDING MYSELF

Dad and Jenna fly home
two days after
the concert.

And the best part is . . .
I go, too.

KATY STAYS

She has indoor
field hockey practice.

And besides, it's time for me
to step out on
my own.

Mom cries when I
hug her at the airport.

Katy does,
       too.

"I'll see you in a week,"
I whisper.

THE VOICE
INSIDE ME . . .

the one that sounds
like Whitney,
knows this is right.

I'm on my way
toward
becoming my own person.

I get on the plane,
notebook in hand,
earbuds in my ears.

This new adventure
is just
the next song
on my playlist.

And I'm finally ready
to live
out loud.

WANT TO KEEP READING?

If you liked this book, check out another
book from West 44 Books:

CATCH ME IF I FALL
BY CLAUDIA RECINOS SELDEEN

Claudia Recinos Seldeen

ISBN: 9781978596351

BALANCING ACT

Hang
on
tight!

When I'm on a trapeze,
I defy gravity.

I'm a leaf
caught in a summer storm.
Twisting.
Spinning.

But there's always that voice
in the back of my mind,
whispering:

Hang
on
tight.

Don't
let
go.

Falling is not an option.

DANCE TRAPEZE

When I tell people
I'm a
trapeze artist,
their eyes
light up
like stars.

I know
they're thinking about
flying
　　　　　trapeze.
About acrobats
w h i z z i n g
through the air.

But
dance
　　　　　trapeze
is
different.

There's no
swinging.
No catching.
No letting go.

A
dance
　　　　　trapeze
doesn't
tick tock
back and forth.

A
dance
        trapeze
spins
in tight circles.

It twirls
and turns.

If you don't hold on,
it will
spin
you
right
off.

NOODLE

After every trapeze class,
I lie on my bedroom floor
and let the bruises
bloom.

That's what
no one tells you
about trapeze.

The bar is made of metal.
The ropes can slip
and burn.

When my mom
calls me for dinner,
I trudge
down
the
stairs
on wobbly legs.

If AnnMarie were here,
she'd call me a
noodle.

She'd flop her arms
like boiled spaghetti
and make me
laugh.
She can
always
make
me

laugh.

But AnnMarie
isn't here.

My best friend
can't come over
on trapeze days.

GETTING IT RIGHT

Angela,
my mother says.
How was trapeze class?

Good,
I answer.
We learned a new drop.

My mother lifts
her head.

*Did you get it
right?*
she asks.

I think of
the drop.
A roll up
into the ropes.
A quick
release.
A dizzying tumble.
Like a snowflake
fluttering
to the ground.
My heart
thundered
when I tried it.

My breath
gasped.
My stomach
dipped.

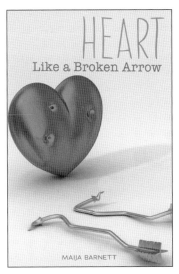

CHECK OUT MORE BOOKS AT:

www.west44books.com

ABOUT THE AUTHOR

Maija Barnett grew up in central Vermont
and now lives in Massachusetts with her
husband and two teenage daughters. She
loves nature, poetry, hiking in the woods with
her dog, and finding ways to get kids excited
about reading. Maija holds degrees in English
and teaching and currently teaches at a school
for students with learning differences.
The Song I'm In is her second novel.